To my future grandchildren and those to come after—
we are all born with a sense of wonder and
excitement and joy. Believe in magic.

A Feiwel and Friends Book

An imprint of Macmillan Publishing Group, LLC

120 Broadway, New York, NY 10271

Our books may be purchased in bulk for promotional, educational, or business use.

Please contact your local bookseller or the Macmillan Corporate and Premium Sales Department at

(800) 221-7945 ext. 5442 or by email at MacmillanSpecialMarkets@macmillan.com.

Library of Congress Cataloging-in-Publication Data is available.

ISBN 978-1-250-26647-7 (hardcover) / ISBN 978-1-250-79728-5 (special edition) / ISBN 978-1-250-80136-4 (special edition)

Book design by Rich Deas and Mallory Grigg

Feiwel and Friends logo designed by Filomena Tuosto

First edition, 2020

10 9 8 7 6

mackids.com

5 MORE SLEEPS 'TIL CHRISTMAS

Jimmy Fallon

illustrated by Rich Deas

Feiwel and Friends • New York

Just **FIVE** more sleeps 'til Christmas.
Can you believe it's here?
I know that Santa's coming soon,
'cause I've been good all year.

5 more sleeps 'til Christmas.
I'm not sure I can wait.

I got good grades,

I fed the dog,

I even cleared my plate.

Gary's chew toy Peppy
is helping me count sheep.
But it's not working! We're still up!
We cannot fall asleep!

Just **FOUR** more sleeps 'til Christmas
and a visit from Kris Kringle!
The halls are decked, the tree is trimmed,
the bells are being jingled.

The cocoa's hot inside the mugs.

The candy canes are crunched.

The popcorn tin is empty
'cause the popcorn's all been munched.

Just 4 more sleeps

and then it's here—

I have to go to bed!

But visions of my

favorite toys

keep dancing in my head.

LETS PLAY THE GAME —
★★★ ★ ★★

ZzZZZZZ

X-mas List
Bike
Guitar
Space
Ship

Now it's **THREE** more sleeps 'til Christmas!
I'm looking at the snow.
I'm watching every snowflake,
thinking "3 more sleeps to go!"

I'm cozy in my bed

with lots of

CHRISTMAS

thoughts to think.

Just **2** sleeps left

when I wake up—

but I can't sleep a wink!

It's **TWO** more sleeps 'til Christmas!

Why can't this day be done?!

If I can get just one more sleep, then we'll be down to 1!

Just **2** more sleeps

to get through! Then

CHRISTMAS DAY

will break.

Just 1 more sleep

plus another sleep . . .

But still I'm

wide awake!

ONE more sleep 'til Christmas!

Is this day finally here?!
I put out Santa's cookies
and the milk for his reindeer.

I'm snuggled in pajamas
and the stockings have been hung.
The tree has been unplugged
and all the carols have been sung.

Just **1** sleep left 'til Christmas!
The day is coming soon!
And can it be?!
I think I saw a sleigh go past the moon!

Today it's finally **Christmas!**
I run down to the tree.
I can't believe it—Santa came!
These gifts are all for me!

MERRY
MERRY
CHRISTMAS!

It's really, truly here!

And now I start
the countdown . . .

Only
364

more sleeps
'til next year!